WALT DISNEY PRODUCTIONS

presents

BAMBI
Grows Up

Random House 🏠 New York

Book Club Edition

First American Edition. Copyright © 1979 by Walt Disney Productions. All rights reserved under International and
Pan-American Copyright Conventions. Published in the United States by Random House, Inc., New York, and si-
multaneously in Canada by Random House of Canada Limited, Toronto. Originally published in Denmark as BAMBI
VOKSER OP by Gutenberghus Bladene, Copenhagen. Copyright © 1978 by Walt Disney Productions.
ISBN: 0-394-84235-9   ISBN: 0-394-94235-3 (lib. bdg.) Manufactured in the United States of America.
90   A B C D E F G H I J K

Thumper the rabbit
ran into the clearing.

"It's happened!
It's happened!" he shouted.
"The new prince has been born."

"The new prince has been born?" cried the owl
from his perch on the old tree stump. "Where is he?
Quick! We must all go see him."

"Follow me!" shouted Thumper.

With a flapping of wings and a pounding of
furry paws, the animals chased after Thumper.
Quick as the wind, they rushed through
the woods to see the newborn prince.

Deep in a thicket, the animals found
the baby prince, lying close to his mother.
The little spotted fawn stared at them
with big, curious eyes.

Then, slowly, he stretched
his front legs and started
to get up.

But his legs wobbled
and slid out
from under him.

The baby prince fell
flat on his stomach.

"A little wobbly, isn't he?" Thumper asked
the fawn's mother. "He doesn't look much like a
prince. What are you going to call him?"

"I think I'll call him Bambi," said the mother.

The fawn stood up again. This time he stayed
on his feet.

His mother looked at him proudly.

Soon summer came, and Bambi was big enough to go walking with his mother.

His legs were longer now—and stronger.

As Bambi and his mother walked under the tall trees, the fawn looked all around him.

Before long, Bambi came to the green meadow.
There he found Thumper, playing with his sisters.

"Come, Bambi!" shouted Thumper.
"Hop over this log with me."

Bambi tried hard to hop over the log,
but he tripped and fell flat on his chin.
"I think you need some hopping lessons,"
said Thumper. "Don't worry. You'll soon
learn how to do it."

Thumper took Bambi to a field covered
with flowers.

Something black and white stuck its nose
out from the midst of the blossoms.

"Is this a flower, too?" asked Bambi.

"A flower! I should say not," said Thumper.
"That's a skunk."

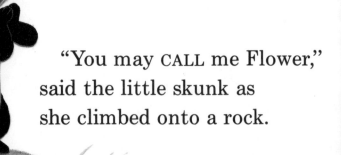

"You may CALL me Flower,"
said the little skunk as
she climbed onto a rock.

While they were talking, something with fluttering yellow wings landed on Bambi's tail.

"Look at that!" said Bambi. "What a beautiful bird!"

"That's not a bird," said Thumper. "It's a butterfly."

Bambi was so happy that he started to run.
Suddenly he came to a pond.
Bambi stared curiously into the water.
He could see another fawn down there.

Slowly he bent
over to rub noses
with the fawn.

BRRR! The water was cold!
He shook his head to get rid of the ice-cold drops.
Then he looked into the water again.
Now Bambi could see TWO fawns!
Who could that second fawn be?

The second fawn was standing right beside him.
She stuck out a leg and shook it at Bambi.
Then she said, "Hi! My name is Faline."

The friendly little prince went up to Faline
and they rubbed noses.

"Bet you can't catch me," called Faline.
And off she ran with Bambi close behind her.
The little prince had made another new friend.

The days passed quickly and autumn
came.

Bambi went for a walk on the
hilltop with his mother.

The air was chilly, and the leaves
had turned red and orange.

"Winter is on the way," said Bambi's
mother. "Soon there will be no more leaves
on the trees, and the hunters will come."

Then Bambi saw a strange, wonderful sight.
Up on the highest mountain peak stood
a great big stag.
    The stag had huge antlers that spread out
from both sides of his head.
    He stood there staring at Bambi.

"Who is that?" asked Bambi. "And why is he staring at me?"

"He is your father," answered Bambi's mother. "He is very brave and very wise."

"Of all the deer in the forest, not one has lived half so long. That's why he is called the Great Prince of the Forest."

Suddenly Bambi heard a loud BANG!
Birds flew by, crying out in warning.
Squirrels, skunks, rabbits, and other animals
rushed past.

"What is it, Mother?" asked Bambi.
"What is happening?"

"Quick, Bambi! Follow me!" said
his mother. "We are in danger. Man
is in the forest."

Safe in a hiding place in the thicket,
Bambi lay close to his mother.

Neither of them moved.

Neither of them made a sound.

Just beyond the thicket stood two hunters
with their guns.

"When man comes into the forest, you must always hide," warned Bambi's mother. "We are all in danger when man is nearby."

One very cold morning, Bambi went walking
with his mother. The ground was covered
with a cold, fine white powder.

"Mother, what is this white stuff?"
asked Bambi.

"It is snow," said his mother. "Winter
has come at last."

"Hi, there, Bambi," said Thumper. "What do you think of the pond now?"

Bambi stared at the frozen pond.

"What has happened to the water?" he asked. "It has a cover over it."

"That is ice," said Thumper. "It's strong enough to walk on. Follow me!"

Bambi followed Thumper onto the ice.

His front feet
slipped one way.

His back feet
slipped the other way.

"Getting wobbly again,
aren't you?"
said Thumper.

The little rabbit grabbed Bambi's hind legs
and tried to help him get on his feet.
"Ice is slippery," said Bambi.

Time passed, and
the snow disappeared.
It was spring again.
Bambi was growing bigger.

The trees had tiny green buds, and fresh
green grass covered the ground.
Flower the skunk had a new family,
and so did Mrs. Quail.

Bambi walked down to the pond to see if the ice was still frozen.

There sat Thumper on a hollow log.

Bambi lowered his head and looked into the water.

"I see a deer down there in the water," he called to Thumper. "It's a buck... with antlers!"

"That buck with antlers is you, Bambi,"
said Thumper. "You have been growing up
during the winter."

Bambi was so proud of his new antlers
that he went off to show them to Faline.
But Faline had met another young buck.
"Hi, Bambi," she said. "This is Ronno."

Bambi was furious.
Why was this strange deer in HIS part
of the forest?
Then, without any warning, Ronno lowered
his horns and charged at Bambi.

But Bambi stood up on his hind legs and struck at Ronno with his hoofs.

He pushed Ronno down the bank into the pond.

Then Bambi came back to Faline.

Proudly, Bambi led Faline out into the meadow.

As he looked up at the mountain peak, he saw his father looking down at him.

The old stag—the Great Prince of the Forest—stared at Bambi with admiring eyes.

The young prince had proved himself to be a brave son.

Bambi had grown up.